OCT 2019

For Elsie and Gloria, such inspiration,
and thanks to Helen.

Ω

Published by
PEACHTREE PUBLISHING COMPANY INC.
1700 Chattahoochee Avenue
Atlanta, Georgia 30318-2112
www.peachtree-online.com

Text and illustrations © 2019 by Julia Woolf

First published in 2019 by Andersen Press Ltd.,
20 Vauxhall Bridge Road, London, SW1V 2SA
First United States edition published in 2019 by Peachtree Publishing Company Inc.

The illustrations were created with mono printing, hand painted, and then digitally colored in Adobe Photoshop.

Printed in February 2019 in China
10 9 8 7 6 5 4 3 2 1
First Edition

ISBN: 978-1-68263-132-4

Library of Congress Cataloging-in-Publication Data

Names: Woolf, Julia, author, illustrator.
Title: Duck & Penguin are NOT friends / Julia Woolf.
Other titles: Duck and Penguin are not friends
Description: Atlanta : Peachtree Publishing Company Inc., 2019. | Summary: Betty and Maud are best friends but their favorite stuffed animals,
Duck and Penguin, are not and do not appreciate being forced to play together.
Identifiers: LCCN 2018061605 | ISBN 9781682631324
Subjects: | CYAC: Stuffed animals (Toys)—Fiction. | Play—Fiction. | Friendship—Fiction.
Classification: LCC PZ7.1.W667 Duc 2019 | DDC [E]—dc23 LC record available at *https://lccn.loc.gov/2018061605*

Julia Woolf

Duck & Penguin are NOT Friends

PEACHTREE
ATLANTA

This is Betty and her favorite toy, Duck.

This is Maud and her favorite toy, Penguin.

"Look how much Duck and Penguin
love each other!" says Betty.
"Kiss, kiss, kiss," says Maud.

Betty and Maud are best friends.

Duck and Penguin are NOT!

Betty and Maud are having a playdate.

First they skip to the swings.

weeeee!!!

Betty pushes Maud
all the way up.

Duck pushes Penguin
all the way off.

whaaa!!

Next, they build sandcastles.
"I love playing in the sandbox," says Betty.

"I bet Duck and Penguin love it too,"
says Maud.

Then, it's time for baking.

"I love cracking the eggs," says Betty.
"I love whipping the cream," says Maud.

"I'm painting Duck," says Betty.
"I'm painting Penguin," says Maud.

splodge!

splodge!

Duck and Penguin are painting each other.

"Now they're all messy!" says Betty. "Duck has paint and sand on him."

"And Penguin has eggs and cream on him," says Maud.

"Nothing better than a good bath to get clean again," says Betty.

"Look at them hanging out together
on the clothesline," says Maud.
"They love each other so much."

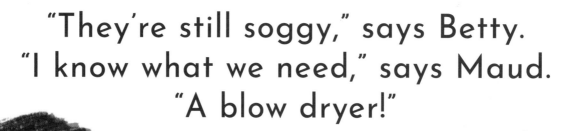

"They're still soggy," says Betty.
"I know what we need," says Maud.
"A blow dryer!"

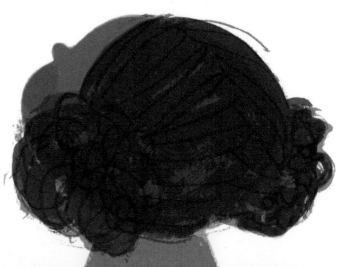

"Not so soggy now,"
says Betty.

"Not so messy
either," says Maud.

"Oh, they're all fluffed up," says Maud.

"They look so cute," says Betty.

"Cute enough to play..."

"Itty-bitty babies!" says Maud.

"We forgot their
bottles," says Betty.

"Let's go and get
them," says Maud.

Duck and Penguin would rather play *anything* besides itty-bitty babies. Yuck!

Swinging,

building
sandcastles,

baking,

and painting are
much MORE FUN.

Quick! Betty and
Maud are coming!

"Here are your bottles," says Betty.

"Look how happy they are," says Maud.
"They really do love each other, don't they?"

And perhaps now, they do.